ELEMENTS & OFFERINGS

ELEMENTS
& OFFERINGS

DAN BEACHY-QUICK

Louisiana State University Press
Baton Rouge

Published by Louisiana State University Press
lsupress.org

LSU Press Paperback Original

Designer: Barbara Neely Bourgoyne
Typeface: Whitman

Cover artwork by Del Harrow.

Cataloging-in-Publication Data are available from the Library of Congress.

ISBN 978-0-8071-8603-9 (pbk.: alk. paper) — ISBN 978-0-8071-8669-5 (pdf) —
ISBN 978-0-8071-8668-8 (epub)

—for Kristy

With just the Door ajar
That Oceans are—

CONTENTS

ELEMENTS & OFFERINGS

The Song Dynasty

—for Seth Braverman, on his thirty-seventh

One way to make snow in mountains is
to leave the paper blank
& ink in the crags & pines—
a scholar's hut by the flowing stream,
such cold water for the tea—
but there are other ways. The mind

makes its equal signs & leaves them
unspoken. A world
much thought about but thinking
leaves no trace. The blankness
snow is to the child
wrapped in her blanket. The snow

there even in June, the summer snow—
I know you know. Imagine
the solstice is a gong that rings out an
echo song—nothing
lasts longer than morning fog. Clouds
can be made just as the snow is made.

& so of mist, vague dews.
So of water dropping off a cliff.
So of the steam curling up
as the cup cools. You leave
the page blank & ink in the dark
dream of pines. Law

of the pines,
the scholars of the Song Dynasty
discovered, painting the world on silk,

on paper. A principle called
Mind, or One. Fire, or
Mite. You

children of snow &
clouds can make snow & clouds
for yourselves. Find
on the blank page some oblivion
& add water to the inkstone. A
drop or two. Begin by painting dew.

An archive.

Library of —

A.

                .

               . .

              . . .

               at

            oms. el

             lips

              es.

             . . .

              . .

               .

B.

Of broken shells—. & the sea—.
There's a book I want to read

but I don't know how to read—.
Venus shines small light on dark loam.

The black-headed gulls—. The wind—.
The waves break open another

page that's not a page. Nothing
here says I alone.

Sea spray—. I heard someone
say the goddess came of—. The foam—.

C.

Of crow logic—

    faith floods the world
    & the fool holds on—.

    A plank across a synapse, a
    board above abyss—.

    Make a nest in virtue—.
    So dearly the dove

    with no grammar does—.
    Empty mouth or olive branch—.

    Where is home when home is

the conditional mood—

    regret flew over the ocean
    but hope flew back

    across the sea—.
    Would, sang the olive branch—.

Could or *couldn't,* said the crow.

D.

Desire is the space between
stars. Distance is
the space within

an apple, a bird, a brain.
A dream of daughters in heaven
diagramming sentences:

The moon is bright. It's not
a light.

Child bent over
a page, erasing nouns
& adjectives, crosses out
all that isn't right:

The, not *a.*

E.

Eider ducks all winter sleep
on the frozen open sea

if these syllables carry care
this blood stays warm as spring

a mind wants to wake up
inside what it builds

a nest on the stones
made of the duck's own down

F.

Forget me not
is whose command to give
the feeling of awe got over me
watching my child lace her shoe the
dog opened his mouth
& in the bee flew

the hard work isn't some agony—

the mouth just opens, the grass just grows—
a tangle in the mind those loose strands
memory pulls the knot tighter
her hair as she runs by a band poorly bound

G.

Of glacial water melted in glass tubes—.
Columns not classical—. Not
holding high the roof beams—.
Of those gods—. For whom light
bends down—.
                    Apollo's temple at Delphi
                    the ruins in memory
                    the columns falling almost all
                    the walls fall down
                    you don't know yourself so much
                    as you thought you did—
                    it remains excessive in the mind—
                    an ancient letter hovering alone

invisible in the air even now
private epsilon of the prophet

E.

H.

Of the hero inside death—
he who has a word has a first principle—
to sing until song doesn't exist.

Moisture in the soil & the seed—
hero who said the earth floats on nothing
as a piece of wood floats on water—

or as an oath sworn floats on the river Styx?
Hero who thought
a stone drawing iron near

had a soul, thought all
things were full of gods. The hero
who, looking up at a star,

fell down a hole.

I.

& the one called Iris is also a cloud,
purple, & yellow, & red to the sight—
& the one called Hana is also a sun, &
the sun is ignited clouds—.

            & the I-It
that is an altar a child made; a column;
a caryatid walking with a fragment of
the temple roof on her head,
offering to others this weight of the sky;
block-tower; girder in the rubble; stalk
of winter wheat; stubble field
of September corn—.
               & the more humble
forms, the lowercase, below us, yet ourselves;
the tree a child draws, green circle on a pencil-
thin line; & dandelion gone to seed—.
                                                   &

the one that makes his wish—.
To have no idea—.

J.

Of Justice who covers her breasts,
turns aside in the kitchen to turn
the radio on. Threatens with furies
the sun if it loosens its measure.
Scents fire with spices & breathes in
the flame. Says the soul speaks
the language of ears & eyes. Says
war is what is shared. Says war is
precedent of all. Says saltwater gives life
to fish but kills a man. Says a donkey lusts
after trash, not gold. Weeping sweeps the
kitchen floor. Says
as child is to father, man is to—. Who

will not say the next word. What is
born from fire to fire returns. All is.
Even night. Even the child's eyes—
even the child she teaches to breathe
under water. Swimming lessons. The principle that
tunes the lyre—. Tunes the bow—.

K.

    Of kings & queens

                    nightly

    they fill

        their chamber pots—.

. . . memories of sentences read years ago: Montaigne's
"On Experience" . . .

    Thinking   truth is not   a
    world or word   apart from this world
    the pain of   the kidney stone
    in the penis   must also be   included

    in the Royal Laws.

L.

Of the lost child, child
who feels her heart's gone missing,
child who wanders from fear far
into the woods, who

makes of leaves a crown to cover
her head, child who chases
the creatures that run from her rule—
white eye of rabbit's tail, green

disc glowing of the deer's midnight eye—
who puzzles out the path
where thought alone makes the nettles tremble
& walks it, child who

enters a cave, discovers the night
is rooted there, & in the husk the sun
dropped as it rose, she makes her bed,
that child, that seed.

M.

My   my
memory my   my mind
the theory   thinks it thinks
my mansion my   home
memory & those   rooms of
closed doors   crumbling walls

for a long time   silence astonished
my heart   my memory cloud
a complex song   eyes
& thunderbolt &   one grain
of millet dropped makes a sound
what is there to think that is

there to think   upload
invoice subject heading no

      attachment
there's the child on a cloud   laughing
there's the child who sings along
there's the child who disappears
when the father writes down   the song

N.

Of noman—
that name is an echo in the blind monster's cave—.

What grammar keeps these ghosts at their labor?

The silent letter *h*—. The silent letter *g*—.

Of gnomon—
the spindle on the sundial that is the one that knows—.
You do your thinking by sunlight or torchlight—. You
make a shadow to see—. But who are you?

Noman. Gnomon. Here's my shadow—.

Tell me what day it is. What day is. What is time.

O.

O limits of the nest
O hidden math of peas in pod
O holy bean field not to be crossed
O honey drone
O torn green scent on fingers

O partial knowledge
O infant tongue
O wisdom stolen from books on loan
O harmonies that make the planets chime
O sty on the child's eye
O violent artificer
O metempsychosis of vegetable soul
O purple aster
O daughter with the tangled hair
O vow of silence
O word of mouth
O torn page of sacred cares

P.

Paths deer find
their own foot formed—

can it be true—
through the thought-tangle—

all—the thinkable
arrives.

Is the burr—my theology—.
Or the thistle—.

I see the sun is
a purple bloom above the thorns—.

I study these hooks
& barbs—.

Q.

Of questions
        no inventiveness
            can find—

        I think
        I'm not thinking
yet. It is

done to me
        what I think
            I do myself.

        Point my finger
        in the passive
tense. Or is it

a mood—. The
        the passive mood—.
            Where is what was

        so near. Deerness—.
        Other thoughts
that leap in fear away

from thinking.
        Is it fear—.
            Or a field—.

        Grass inside a
        question. No
idea is as green.

R.

—of rituals of purification, of the root-bearing fields, of
the right hand as a leaf held up to the sun,
of resonance, of desire, of Roman rings found in
urns shattered by the plow, of raccoons
stealing minnows from the bait can in moonlight, of
rest & restless dreams, of her robe's loose knot, of
love & strife & restoring back to life
a woman who stopped breathing, of a voice
calling a name through the air, of a philosopher
walking to the volcano's edge & jumping in,
of theories of return, of resurrection, of recognition,
of being or becoming a god, of ash, of recorded memory, of
a bronze sandal found after the mountain erupts,
of repeated lessons in old books, of the child
who calls herself goddess of rainbows, of the child
reading song lyrics on her glowing screen,
of relative motion, of memory in the recursive mind, of
seed-sown rows, of seeds planted in the runnels of
the ears, of conference registrations, of rectitude, of
religious mystics & their beds of stinging nettles, of
rent overdue, of realization, of harmony as glue—

S.

Sun & countersun
is what is sayable what is
said or unsaid or do vaster
entanglements wreck the sum
of love & strife &
that fire around which
the human eye gathers

the adequate idea is
angles with no passion
God's own geometry
a lantern behind veils
keeps its flame a flame
the subconscious flicker
the lit wick stays blind
in wind &/or at night

T.

Of time
          the ancient scholars agree
it created itself
          it was not
created

it makes personal the condition life
          calling itself life

but we say time
          in secret to ourselves

U.

un-

          negates

um-

          pauses

*

I wanted to think about the universe.
    How it came to be.
How in it there are rabbits, stars, memories, children.
    I wanted to think about others thinking
how thought is the blood around the human heart.
    I found in myself old fears; only some of them were mine.
What is thought about turns away from thinking.
    What is spoken about turns away from words.
I wanted to find the proper invocation.
    Not the goddess to sing wrath; not the god to sing power.
Word that opens within itself an honest void.
    A mind nest; a house of brooding.

*

unum
unum

V.

Of atoms in the void
where the monads assemble memory—
you beetle dark as the wild carrot's one dark petal you
Pythagorean theorem you proof on a page
you principle running naked down the hall you wife you
child wandering the dunes
the cask can hold the wine but also the wineskin the wine was in
& so of the child's first philosophy
putting her head in the water letting breath escape her lips
the bubbles that rise through the element

demonstrate the quiet work of that god named fear
who sets in motion those atoms that would not move
rising from heart to mind a face inside each or is that love
the god named love or the god named thought
I thought a little knowledge would help me
as wings help sparrows I thought open books could fly
but I'm not a child I don't get out of the water & cry

W.

Of the letter *w*
who sometimes on silent wings

     wren
         write

nests in the eye but not in the ear

     holy homonym
         & sacred ritual

of how to disappear in plain sight

X.

Let X equal a man.
For many years, X has dreamed of tornadoes—first
   in fear, then of wanting the wind to hit him.
Once X dreamed lightning struck
   his right hand, but he woke to no scar.

Twice in his life X dreamed about heaven—first,
    not knowing how he'd died, he walked into a
    green field where others wandered, some of
    whom he recognized; he met his wife in that
    meadow; she was still alive.
    In the next dream heaven was a mountain lodge
    with dark wainscoting, & one of the guests
    warned X that it can get so boring that you can lose
    your mind, pointing out a man
    staring at a small refrigerator.
X dreamed he was a dolphin swimming under a river covered
    by ice, & his wife was a hawk flying above him.
X dreamed a child & the child came true—
    the child fell asleep & dreamed about a cricket
    in the desert.
Let Y equal the child.
For X some books he's read stay in him as do dreams
    & uncertainly remembered things:
Like the page that spoke of one's life being a sentence
    an invisible pencil writes at night—
    & the sentence that the sun is an eternal fire within us.
X had another child—it's true.
She's real, X tells himself.
X knows there's a problem to solve; for a long time he
    desired to solve it himself, but he couldn't learn
    how to think.
Now X knows he's part of the problem.
In the dream he hasn't yet had, the moon is his teacher,
    & she writes in chalk
    on the night-dark blackboard, *Solve for X.*

Y.

Why? asks the child—
I agree, but the answer's wrong.
Later she says: *Yesterday is yellow.* Eating
the sun-yolk of an egg. Trying to
remember the question.

*

Why me? asks the child,
   hardly a child anymore.

My lyric register needs some repair. You,
I say, I want to say, you—

but the pronoun grows vague.

Z.

Of zero—

      the air within it thinks
      as the hot air inside the sun also thinks—

      it is great, powerful, eternal,
      immortal & possessed
      of wide knowledge—

      it creates a bound around all
      within it, marking love's outermost limit, erasing
      itself by establishing
      the innermost distance:

Final sum the numbers reach—.
Even those numbers, the gods—.

Of Zeno—

    sitting on a stone
    behind my eye, teaching me
    my prayers:

    Let Achilles lose the stadium footrace—.

    Let the shot arrow be still in the air—.

A braid of.

Elemental

To clear conceals—
every act of clearing

every nearing
endures a new form of
distance it tries

to endear—wisdom is
learning not to listen
so as to overhear

the accidental
world speaks itself asleep

Auricle

—for Sasha Steensen

No lamb I know asks
    the question—
but I only know one lamb.
Though the coal burns
    bright orange
behind the dark iron
slats, no tiger I know
    asks—
but I don't know any tigers.
When the child misspells
    good as *god*
I correct her. You need
another *o*. Oh, she says,
    okay. A dog
with no legs and no tail
sleeps on her throat
    at night.
A lamb lies down
under the yellow stars
    printed
on her sheet. She never
asks, either. Silent as her
    pet lamb. Okay?
Silent as her tiger that can't
bother to exist.

Inf—, inf—

some know what I know
what over the poppy fields they carry
gold not only a rumor but a weight
that makes flight harder
and makes it harder to fight

does it at night make you sad or do you ask
children how does it work
the bullet loaded with pollen and the hollow
point a flower makes
about the sun when it opens

Elemental

not knowing how to speak is is
not knowing how to listen

is is

the little gold, the large earth

Auricle

They must grow so tall
    before they look down—
        narcissus, my

paperwhite children.
    A button turns on the fire
        in the morning's quiet dark.

I read some words out loud
    in my head, *the always*
        filling never full sea.

I gathered them around me
    to ask if they believed
        in fate. None of those faces

raised a hand, those faces
    in my dream. A single strand
        of Hana's hair hangs off the gentle

blossom. I see it in the fire light,
    hanging there. Cut by no shear.
        It just fell down through the air.

Inf—, inf—

maybe the facts are only rumors each one
whispering behind its own back that it doesn't exist

infinity, infantry

the witness knows but won't say
points at his mouth and makes certain motions
so everyone knows his mouth doesn't work anymore
not the way his mouth used to work

maybe they just repeat what they're told

the fact is I don't exist
the inner life is another myth

Elemental

What in the eye is clear the
ear mistakes—

a world that is world for all—

wisdom is what keeps words
away from thinking

too close the names—

planets caught in heaven's circles
glow, or are they empty bowls
filled with fire—

the stars don't know

Auricle

I listen and listen but how do I know
  Peace Peace in the plural says please or pleads
I hear the whole song divide the state as one
  appeals past the last centuries' pealing bells
wren under eaves ruins another wren's heaven
   dying sympathies appear as a pear or peas
with her territory her tune I want a nest
  clinging to the twine Please Please in the plural
not a flag a mead hall not a circumstance
   puts pain's poor plea deeper in the apparent
a stable not a stability where animals dream
  pressure the day lily plant the possible prayer
and dreaming among them I tell the stranger
   pulling apart the sepal petals by their dusty crease
in my mind I can't I don't know how to sing

Inf—, inf—

some eyes see through walls some special eyes
see something like a ghost float over and bend down

lift into light a lesser light some eye sees
both merge into one and glow brighter

but an eye can't pull a trigger a finger does
    infrared

a bone commands obedience
even the clouds obey and let the message through

Elemental

The mind and every
creature driven to pasture by blows—

first water, then fire
then strife, then atoms, then logic,
then the long truce of grass—

it returns well fed and strong
to keep me away from myself—heart's

old chaos—

closes behind it the gate it is
itself the gate—

mind the world meadows

Auricle

Knot the mind—

    fear no good
      at finding its edges—.

Not the mind—.

    Sudden sullen
      architecture—
    I have a

wall and no heart—.

Inf—, inf—

the glowing red bundle crawls across the screen playing
with a red ball that can't be seen

how long an object holds the heat
of the hand that held it
depends on the hand and the object

and time

time blurs the glowing trace
it disappears as a finger is just a flame that burns

on a wick of bone it burns

Elemental

one
dies to become another one

motherless the atoms

the earth is good and
bad

the stupid don't see what they see—
the blind see more—

the voice that calls me dumb
comes from the sun—

Auricle

Out the cloud a voice spoke to us to us
the voice said make no images

a crocodile a boat a rocket ship look up
there's mom there's you there's an ant a snake a shoe

says the child looking up at the clouds
says the child looking up at the clouds

I never saw the sun I thought the sun
was a fire the shadows fed the flame in the cave

and when every leaf on the tree became a mirror
the tree burst into light I couldn't see myself

until I stepped nearer and nearer and
among the leaves I found the dark cave again

and rehearsed what I'd learned—fighter jet
and drones, bees and honey, elections and stones,

the screens fill up each year with the never-yet-seen
end of the world or is it the edge where is the edge is it where

Agamemnon walks down the red carpet to take a bath
or some other scene—Achilles barefoot before his boat

singing a song to no one who's listening—
so shiny the metal reflects the hand that comes

to grasp it and the statue gets darker that way—
the winners take home their man made of gold

Inf—, inf—

what falls from brightness isn't it also bright
pollen maybe and these petals that hide the wound

or the litter of the stars those bright tissues
the gods wipe their eyes when they laugh so hard

they cry and drop the refuse down
in the dark where beauty overtakes us who look up

to study it all is to become less
then ignorance doesn't work so well anymore

can't get so small it cancels my life but I feel it
the gap as it nears waking the similes like like

Elemental

Throws its square
on the bare wall

where in the little square of light
I think of the little square of light—

a kind of emptiness or is it
the sun's discarded geometry,

not subject to, not object of—

someone becomes the beginning
every day of his own desire,
or is it his demise—

as a tree becomes an apple
and truth, a tooth

Auricle

The wind changed me
    Into a deer, the same
Wind blowing the army away
    Blew away my father.
I like being a deer. I eat
    The grass that is my altar.
In the morning the clouds
    Fill up the trees. Sometimes
The trees fill up the sky.
    A thin gold chain
The goddess made she clasped
    Around my neck.
So I came to the holy grove.
    I sacrificed my name.

Inf—, inf—

like my heart has ears like my mind has hands
but mostly the confusion ends

life is or isn't brief
full to the extent that contains it

like
like the breath in the bubble the child blows

prayer goes up and up
mindless and not in control of itself

through the gaps in the branches the night still
works all right still is dark and still parts shine

and though it bursts don't pay it any mind
air melts into air painlessly

I call it anesthesia but I say it time

Elemental

I searched myself—
for a river, for some earth—
but what loves to hide

hides
even me from myself hides

as I believe the
clouds hide their harm deep

living the sun's death
and the cloud's being dead is
the other's life—

is the other's life, life—
the riddle comes as a circle—

the heart is a circle
is a thought the brain thought

it thought

Auricle

No reference
  so I read the cricket
song
  that grass page
in the dusk of—
  in the dust at—

the mouth
  of the mine
memory
  made claim

I've forgotten
  at night sometimes,
sometimes
  all day
if I am still my own or what
  is mine—

it's hard to know
  where to begin
when there is no
  first page—

the moon
  lights up like a page
then the cloud
  hides it—
or

  in the cold ash
to draw a circle
  around the fallen-
through-the-
  smoke-hole sun

Inf—, inf—

the critics called it pathetic but I kept on
the stars couldn't all be wrong
and the poems that picnic in eternity
and the rushes that in the heart grow up big and sing

three times I called out to *recipient unknown*

give me a task to bend down my head
       as the wind tasks the reed
       it touches its tongue to water to sing

and give me love that's weak no more
       that in deep water
       seeks no shallow no shore

Elemental

The limit is there
inside doom like this labor of
serving the one you rule—

self, child—

time plays checkers
to pass time—

breath kindles and puts out
the brightnesses of eyes

Auricle

. . . in the car with my mom as a child in the white
Ford Escort stick shift the first car she bought
years after the divorce with a radio unlike the orange
Datsun B210 that worked I remember how the dial
glowed when the headlamps turned on I would kill
the silence when I turned the tuning knob to the right
an amplified click when the speaker stuttered on
and not the music but the dialing slowly across
the frequency the orange line would between numbers find
voices just out of reach just a syllable from grave distances
or a phrase that within the eerie static articulated love or
the weather or the victory of the local team sometimes the
names of minor heroes
and sometimes time itself and sometimes the crime
report and those voices seemed to me to speak from
out of some pain I knew existed but could not feel
myself some long-ago ever-yet-to-be storm where
blown apart by desire and by desire blown together
the voices neared to tell their story to be
remembered by someone even a kid curled up
in the dark space beneath the glove compartment
shying away whenever the signal became so strong the
song clarified its backbeat in the air dialing away
from the oldies and the news trying so hard to listen . . .

Inf—, inf—

but blood beats so loud it deafens
deafens from within

but brightness stays in the eye long after
long after the bright thing is gone

philosophy is right to be skeptical

of song so good at pointing out certainty
won't last long

Elemental

Sleepers at work
in the common law—

a fire there of their own
making masks solitude
as light, as heat—

dark conjures a world
no one shares, a heart
to climb into and close

behind, a voice—
a man calls his child, child—

the terror-marvels, those gods
call him baby

Auricle

Using god's own language to describe god's face
        paint by number
where each number is a god
                the child never stops learning
on her fingers to count to the number ten
        decades of eternity
                lodged in the mortal circuit immortal
in the capillary's lace heat nervous thought

a mistake can paint the sky that green of child's grass so
        the grass must be
                the sea in this version
of the world it doesn't mean god is less godlike
        but lives inside the fallible
                architecture of Mount
Parnassus whose height hovers whole in the synapse

but also the child who notices the light changes its
        answer depending on
                the question she asks it
also the child in the unified field plucking stem
        by stem the grass
                and weaving a green
blanket so small only two bees could sleep under it

little father little mother let me sing the work song so
        the work gets done
                the dot to dot and
the word search the line that crosses out and the line
        that connects the crocus
                to Orion's bright heel
and lowercase i to the dance in the innermost hive

the paper page to the wasp's chamber to the monocle
       worn by the minister
             of finance to the hole
in the mortar between bricks where the mud dauber lives
       strung tight
             the intervals ring
inside the labyrinth ear and make the monster sigh

Inf—, inf—

weak as a child's grasp but it's what I have
a syllable I say called *all*
it's like one beat of the heart and the other
beat won't follow

and so the lake inside my chest fills up
with blood maybe forever
or do I have it backwards in this song
and the lake is a river emptying

beat

and it won't stop

Elemental

Inside the sun every day
irises rise
initiates to the green inch—

and there are other mysteries
not your own—

a small death mixed in with wine
and the dragonfly catching fire

but what is known is not
always holy—

praying to images as if the
image was not a stone

washing the body in mud
or blood

muttering the word atone—

apology is not the star's tune

Auricle

argue ague ago a
        I knew a child who lost like
the dandelion blown
        language a letter at a time

seed cede ceased ease
        I knew a field that grew
like the wild carrot wild
        intimate of intricate absence

world o wold word old
        I knew a man with a mind
like the canary in the mine
        sang out diamond sang out gold

Inf—, inf—

my neck is sore from trying but still I try
just to keep turning my head around behind me
just to see and to look up because I—

thought I heard a rumor in a syllable in a cloud
saying child over and over again
like wind says once forever because the word once

was spoken o master o known unknown

Elemental

Those gods, those goods, they go
drifting through my stupidity—

the wind lifts a little
her hair that hangs before her eyes
my daughter—

the dog barks at him he doesn't
know—

a fool at every word I flutter—

there is too much of this
life of which

there is never enough

Auricle

Your world seems to stand next to the world.

Your image waits to be seen.

Your night wakes up into another kind of dream.

Your body is made of holes you don't know how to fill.

Eyeholes that fill with whiteness and that hunger-hole.

You are the space in which the event called you occurs.

To say more is sacrilege.

But there are other definitions, you child of wonder.

A bee not yours climbs into the open lily of your mind.

Inf—, inf—

close my eyes and ears close the drone
if you close the sky I'll close the book
there are some other bargains I can make
but not many end in so much that's blank

white noise chatter oracle's friendly fire
command doesn't care if it doesn't matter

like an image I'm learning how to like you
like a fact I mimic want
see all this desire I keep hidden in my mouth

it says love love and so I must learn to learn
about truth I must learn to be less than true

& offerings.

Prosody

—for Ann Lauterbach

The lamb couldn't become an iamb
    much to my sorrow, much
to the lamb's relief. My teacher said
    the ocean hid in anapests,
in the lull of the wave, in the lull
    of the prepositional phrase—
in dreams bright children drown
    diagramming sentences,
dependent on a dependent clause
    for rudder through the rapids,
mesmerized by the solar asterisk
    spinning in the eddy with the
gathering foam, dimly aware
    something remains to be said,
in a, of a, for a, with a, for a, of a, in a field of
    asphodel their mothers
hear from the dark room's open door
    in the middle of the night.
Or just one child. Just his mother.
    Just that bedroom an earthquake
could destroy, or a fire burn, just
    that room where, behind closed
eyes, the fire burns, the earth shakes,
    and not a book falls off the shelf,
and not a page is aflame, though
    in the air the scent is singe of
the moon on fire once again.
    In a cave a goddess in echoes
sobs at her son's fate as her son
    walks into the ocean to wash
the blood from his wrath. Imagine
    in dactyls what the hand can do,

it still can do and does worse
    than imagining can fathom.
It can be gentle, too. The mind
    couldn't become pyrrhic,
much to my sorrow, much to my
    delight. The horse galloping
now in green trochees across the field
    also beds down in a meadow
unseen, its haunch flinching in dream.
    Quickened at external relations,
the heart has its spondees that slow blood
    down into thought, thought slows
down into memory so vivid it feels, as you
    draw hand to chest, your heart
might stop beating. But it's just an idea
    of death. Not death itself. Not
that drone inside silence so different
    than chaos, like the blueshift
of quasars inching backward through
    time, like the sun in bronze
on an ancient ring, or a bee hanging
    golden on a hook within the ash
within the urn. The pollen won't
    quit gathering inside the poem.
Subject to what does not exist,
    my teacher told me to submit.
The mind-wings hum in tune, in time.
    Mother, all I want is honey in a hive.

The No-Thing Nothing Is

—for Kylan Rice

Death came before life ended,
    a fever in the lowercase ill *a*
that *b* fearfully describes as a silence
    that tried to, but couldn't, survive.

The stars predicted the *o*
    would ripen into a green olive,
& the philosopher talking in his sleep
    recites the alphabet, a love poem

to all he could not know. Life came
    before death ended, a fever
in the uppercase Z, & the blind prophet,
    after a sip of blood, spoke of another

letter he couldn't pronounce, but pulling
    from his pocket a fig, pointed at it—

pointed at it, the fig he pulled from his
    pocket, mouthing the words, *if only—*

Love: An Essay

—for Forrest Gander

A poet I love cautions against closure
    but the night ends the day and then does so again.
A philosopher I love has no faith that the sun
    that rose today will rise tomorrow;
    when a student answered wrong the problem
    in math he boxed her ear to bleeding; there's no guarantee.
A person I love dislikes poems written about writing poems; she
    is the broken temple whose oracles say *Know not yourself.*
Another poet I love was found in the afterlife crying out tied
    naked to a brass pillar near another poet I love found
    hanging from a tree and surrounded by snakes.
Another philosopher I love blames the poets for their lies;
    he'd banish them from the ideal city, but would be willing to die
    many times to talk with Homer and Hesiod; this philosopher
    died in a prison writing poems.
A poet I love felt so ashamed of talking too much at a party
    that he didn't let himself look at the sunset as he walked home.
A teacher told me to make friends with the dead.
A child I love said she wanted to live on the mountain made
    of clouds and be a construction worker there.
Something overtakes the mind that wants reversal.
A poet I love desired sensation more than thought
    but in the end could feel nothing but the sensation
    of dying; the idea of a rose has no scent; even thoughts
    die.
Fleeing from philosophy, one philosopher I love struck the ear of
    his student so hard her eardrum burst; he said,
    "Ethics and aesthetics are one."
Something overtakes the mind and obliterates beauty.
A teacher closed her eyes at the end of class and spoke in lament.
A child I love fell asleep in my arms saying, *A cricket*
    in the desert, a cricket in the desert, a cricket which can only be found
    by its song.

A philosopher I love says happiness is the soul at work.
A poet I love held her soul against a screen, and so she learned to see;
 she learned something about the heart hard to convey:
 it's a bullet pulsing in a chamber.
A man I met in a dream told me I must learn to cut the sword in half using
 nothing but the sword.
Something silent overtakes the mind when it reaches a limit.
A poet I've read gave up writing poems after discovering
 how beauty worked against truth; she began work on a dictionary.
Sometimes the mind is overcome with the sensation of thought.
A poet I love wasted away in confusion
 or he stumbled and hit his head on a rock
 because he couldn't solve the fisher-boys' riddle;
 "lice" was the answer;
 he's been dead so long he may never have existed.
A person I love sends photos of the wood he's cut and stacked;
 he never found a use for art; his son became a poet;
 now he calls this work his art.
Something like mortality comes near the mind and it retreats
 into a method.
A poet I love wrote about a tree that grows behind the eye; he
 waters it with his fears,
 which is a quiet lesson about the nature of tears.
"Please, O God" is a way many prayers begin.
A good method can execute itself almost all by itself
 like dreaming is a method in the diamond mine called darkness or
 mind.
"O Muse, sing to me" is a way many poems begin.
A poet I love has a soul that inscribed on her skin "Not at home";
 before she died she wrote in a letter, "Called home."
A friend I love who is a poet I love wakes up every day to
 realize her mother is still missing; a euphemism keeps
 sacred the secret it doesn't say.

Another poet I love said that sometimes God is the light
    beneath the crack of a hotel door, and sometimes God
    is nothing at all.
Something overtakes the mind that learns it can't make reversal work.
One response is to think endlessly in the same way in the same direction.
Another response is to stop.
Sometimes fear so overtakes the mind it wants to hide what all it loves.
Other times it just wants to make a list and count the tally up.
One of the philosophers I love doubts what it means
    when someone says, "I know this is my hand"; but
    it's just as hard to doubt this is my hand;
    this philosopher wants to know what such doubt feels like.
Something called doubt grows overtakeless in the mind given
    over to memory or to thinking.
A philosopher I love was in the habit of playing by the river
    a flute which made no sound, so the song sounded like the river; at
    his sister's funeral he played a music box;
    it sounded like no earthly tune.
A colleague told me a story about a young man who arrived
    at his defense wearing a collar he made into a Mobius strip;
    the student said it was a reminder.
I know I wrote this poem by hand. But I know "by hand" is
    euphemism for some other process.
This work of learning how in "singing not to sing" so
    different than knowing.
Something overtakes the mind that wants what it fears.
Overtakes the mind that wants to continue.
Overtakes the mind that wants to forget forgetting.

Elegy

—for Alesia Tyree

Autumn's first frost recalls the eon-ache of an endless June,
the ceremony hidden in the teacup of the letter *u,* warming
the hand that holds it, & lowercase *n* reminding us
the ceremony ends, teacup rinsed, washed, left to dry
upside down on a dishtowel, *un-* the quiet prefix in the air,
unsettling the wary dog who cocks her ear at a footstep,
unable to fall asleep beside her who sleeps in the rocking chair.
Outside the first flowers that bloom had bloomed—
the crocus comes to mind, but the plans are for other flowers
more resplendent in the eye, a bird-of-paradise, a bird-of-
paradise . . . & it's so often the case, then as now, that a shadow
darting across the sidewalk or the neighbor's grass is what
compels you to look up, an instinct not a choice, mouth agape
with some word about to be said, but it stays unsaid, unsaid,
as the rock doves winging circles round the bell tower
fly suddenly away into other hours, hours no longer ours,
& the cardinal in the crabapple sings out its bright notes, counting
as a child counts her fingers, one to ten & back again, almost forever.

Shepherd of —

—for Donald Revell

invisible anchors of the bright bright clouds
and the bent-over grasses with the unseen sails
the stones that endure without vision
and the swarm's all-mind no-mind patient dance

none else can dance the commandments less-than
more-than-real warnings of the double mind's deathly
advice / / that the elm also bears fruit by bearing
the fruitful vine and the jar half empty worries the mind
to make vinegar from wine / / listen now and understand

these visions build a fence around the vineyard
so trespass becomes the holy guard
keeping none out not child not deer not mouse / /
the shepherd makes such sanctuary in a fold

While Reading Robert Duncan in a Meadow

—for Mai Wagner

the Law-giver   it's on those words
the carpenter bee lands
darker than its shadow the morning sun
demands outgrow the life
that casts it   life that by itself builds its shadow
shadow that describes the life   almost exaggerates
as the shadow mouth seems to sip the hidden
nectar in the word
stamen of the lowercase *i*

and the shadow of the wing is a kind of
shade   a kind of window
kind of dark-lit threshold arch gateway to—

    I heard no sound of hammers and nails
        when from the book the bee flew away

A Late Exam at the River Lethe

—for Martin Corless-Smith

doing math in the sum-light
kept misspelling good as god   minus 1 point
me did this   minus 1 point   not I   minus
another

confused adams with atoms   the eternal
table of adams   hydrogen
lighter than air is the first element   the second
is hydrangea a heavy blue heavier

than the sky hidden behind the garden walls
called   minus 2 points   paradise
then helium and thus the yellow balloon on fire
that is the sun   and hiding inside

the sun is a grid the eye must become
so patient to see the darker
orange separate from the brighter   so patient
seeing is   minus 1 point   going blind

in the architecture of morning light   my head is
hands and feet   considering a simple square
a floor with a door and a bed with a book
a mosquito in the air misquoting Homer

wrath and wandering   in her high-pitched
bloodthirsty   minus 1 point   no-mercy-hum
the mind does move it is a damselfly eclectic blue
from reed to thought to memory

of what's been read   a poem
no one's mouth wrote one thousand years ago
earthe toc of earthe earthe with woh   syllables
that make the self sayable   minus 2 points   I

came into the world by climbing out the cave
minus 1 point   the cave I think it was
my mouth   a soul is like a breath or is it like
wind   minus

1 point   always leaving behind the fact
as if it didn't matter   of the wound the mouth is
another myth ajar   minus 1 point   a mouth is a jar
for breath and breath's   scent: twine, thyme, time

Life Sentences

—for Srikanth Reddy

You must climb the ladder made of light
Thrown by the shutter slats on the wall
And that's not all—.
                Must paint—
Who doesn't?—on the ceiling of your cell
A blue sky, a cloud in jail.
                Then begins
That sound scraping against the floor,
The tap against the wall, that looking
For a door
        When you must for yourself
Be a blindman's cane—.
              Looking is
Not the right word.
            Where is your war
Chest, your greaves, your shield?
                Where
Is your child, that pile of leaves, the empty
Cigar box with the unpaid bills?
              The dark
Behind closed eyes is a different dark—
No chaos, no desire, no midnight reprise
Of the voice that said
          I want you.
It's not darker. There's just more dust,
More memories of clouds
            From which lions
Roared down, and other sounds—
Rain on roof, mouth on pillow bitten down,
Moth on window flying to moon.
             No god came

To tell me it's too soon to start
The complaint, the appeal—. Somehow I know
The latent law of—.

                      The metronome—.

Every separation is a link, says
The tapping in the other room—

                            All the rooms—.

I can and I can't open these eyes
I must open—.

                Endure, endear—.

I want you, too—.

            To open—.

                    My mouth—.

Or a mouth—.

            Any mouth—.

                To open—.

These imperatives of parole—.

•

Sense Without Sense of —

—for William Currey

A man shoulders his burden, and he can't
Say himself what he carries.

A book. A bundle of sticks. Or
He is himself what he carries. A spark.

A description of a spark. A moth
Carrying her dust to the moon

Flies across the field
Of vision, drawing

Your eye away from its occupation. Not
Revelation. Or contemplation.

Some form of opening the eye
Wider. He is still there, the man,

Making by hand an obscure thing,
Muttering to himself in the gathering dark

Songs his mother used to sing—
Not his mother, the moth-ur, the ur-moth—

Some songs about the moon.
He's hard to see, and you cannot

Hear him, this man maybe you are,
Or were, or could be. So central

Once to our story, he seemed a hero.
Now we've gotten nearer the fact

He is more distant, more true—
True, he carries inside himself some fragment

Of the sun. True, he is for us
As a word written in a language we can read

In the margin of a book we cannot.
Let it be enough. Let it be a kind of proof.

Kintsugi/Ostraca

—for Del Harrow

Hidden in what it hides
Flaw time finds buried inside itself
What all time buries
The potsherd waiting in the pot
The hole in the urn and the burial plot

Crack beneath the celadon craze
In blue and white a crack in the scholar's gaze
A blue and white river, a blue and white tree
The surface is the limit of the made thing
A brush paints in the distance to the far mountains

But the distance hides within
All the work it takes to build a hole
Time doesn't know how to do it
emptying what's empty
To a surface atom-thin cerulean and gray

Then there's the damage that can be gilded
Gold lacquer gold coil or staple made of gold
Genius keeps repairing the decay of things
But no gold or god can fill the hole
The shard dropped in doesn't make silence whole

B____ & T____

—for Marius Lehene

I am inside the world & the world is
inside me. & it used to be a comfort
to recite to myself some simple words—
"The world is what is at hand." Hammer,

flower, brick, the bee—it depends so much
on the occasion—chicken, wheelbarrow,
rain. But the hammer abuts the plank, plank
the sill, sill the window's leaden glaze—& then

through the window, the gaze. That's when
the hand comes all by itself to the lips
as if to feel the words before they're spoken.
A memory of looking through another window

years ago, beyond the peas and garlic, a skunk
beneath a tree. Milky Way's white stripe

*

across the sky's dark hair—I know you're there
still, somewhere in the innerworldly. There

where the hand can touch the skin, but not
what is within. Idle talk in idle rooms.
Curious entanglements hearsay knots
into the tangle of the everyday every I

I am tangles me in tighter. Then there is
nothing that is not at hand, & nothing
of any use. What can be found only as it flees?
A leaf falling through the apple tree

hitting other leaves as it falls down.
What is the threat, so near it's already here,
taking away your breath—it's here—
yet it's nowhere—that sound—.

Homeric Philosophies

—for Sally Keith

By thistle-light the bedroom glows.
A thought of home inside the bone.
Ocean cave of open mouth.
Love herself rides a horse through the ocean.
Wisdom lays herself down in bed to read
An epic poem shooting arrows at waves.
This thistle is the phosphorous ideal:
Erotic hum of the mind's silent um,
Rough breath that is the letter *H*
The ancient grammars occasionally deny.
For centuries grammar denies Love herself
Rides her horse across the ocean.
Wisdom sleeps in a cave and dreams
There is a poem yet to be written named Home.
The healer is searching for a wound.
The sea the sea. The bone the bone.
Both are inside me when I read the words.
The book lends my life from the library
Or my life is the book on loan.

A Moon, a Mother, a Moth, a Mouth

—for KBQ

Let the moon be your guide
    of how, night by night, to grow
some emptiness and climb inside
    and make there a little home
to brood on matters silently:
    the moth that mothers you
when your mouth can't say
    how it is you love what you love:
even your children's bright faces
    have their dark sides
the moon minds and reminds:
    memory is the other mother
who loves with you what you love
    most: the silence before
or after someone has spoken certain
    words: love's brooding labor
that loosens the tongue into heavy wings:
    song isn't what sings: the moth
flies out the mouth and knows what to do:
    life isn't what you get to choose
but a light held aloft above you, calling
    you home: not "come home":
telling you your name is home.

Memory–Wax, Knowledge–Bird

—for R. C. Quick

I saw him in the summers when the leaves were green.
Down by the lake where ivy covered the ground. Where
The dogwood's new pale moon flowers browned
At the edge by brittle June. I saw him then
Fishing for lake trout, throwing the sunfish too bony
Back. The sun moved across the sky, around the Earth,
A day, a day, and bees, those day laborers, heaved
Pollen and carried a sting, and bore on their gleaming
Backs a stripe of day and a stripe of night, of night,
A robber moon, thief of her own life, and in the hive
Round as the moon, they locked the work of the field
Away in wax vaults, food for Time to eat some other
Time, the bees.
                    In the fall I went away to where I lived
The year. He'd walk the changed woods gathering
Leaves no longer living—cast in the color shroud
Of no one's weaving—a brighter thought thinks
The goldfinch dull, though the cardinal pretends
Not to notice or know—and taking death's small portion
Home, dipped the leaves in paraffin wax. Let them dry.
Let them cool. Put them in a department-store box
And sent them through the air to my home.
                                        Look:
I could be there with him in the woods in no other
Way. No other path led to the maple leaf's dying-sun
Red larger than my hand that held it. No other path
Led to the oak leaf's cinder-glow-below-dark-ash
Orange. The dark-faith-sunspot-hours of yellow
Beech. The minutes-of-green-flame-faith buried
Within the darkening love of the almond leaf.
Leaf by leaf I took them out and put them on
The floor, and when there was no more, I put
Them back in the empty box, fit on the lid, and hid

New memory in the closet with the other dead
Years.
          Closet where as a child I hid myself and hid
My fears. From where in the night I could hear
Voices speak my name, could hear a song play
On a cylinder of wax, a violence, a violin, a piano
Note beneath the static and the static like a heartbeat
Throbbed, like a sudden wind blown through
The mind-tree's wax-covered leaves, a wind
That suddenly dies—the voices, they were legion,
The chorus in the blood, mumbling out the grave
Delay, gravel on the cemetery driveway, the stones
Time wears away, time wears away their names.
Listen:
          Child-no-longer-young who used to play.
Dipping finger in the candle wax and peeling it off
Like another skin. The fingerprint lit up by flame.
Melting it. Doing it again. And that other finger.
The one not yours. The one not seen by anyone.
That finger that pressing down on the mind's hard wax
Softens it. Then there is nothing that won't
Make its impression—sun-script on small waves,
Sun-page on flat stone, sun-shaft shot down
Through the canopy-maze of the dark leaves,
The bright spot on the ground. And more. More
Faces. The people I love. Strangers. The music
Of their least-thought words—*the baby's sleeping
With his mouth open; I don't think that's how you spell it; the
Weatherman got it wrong*—helplessly recorded
On the wax-hemisphere until so many voices
Overlap no single voice remains. Not a chorus.
A chaos. A static. A hum.
          And then some voice

Asks you what you think.
                              And then some voice
Asks you to think:
                              I think the beehive looks like
The full moon that lights it up—the mind says
To itself—I think the child's hand is an oak leaf—
A theory—what the soul says to itself—is thinking—
So many leaves—the eye says to itself—from trees
Fall down into the wax—I know—the edges
Touch and the wax melds—and I don't know—
The leaves together—what I know—can't be told
Apart—says the tongue to itself—all by itself—
What I know I can't tell—I can't pull it apart—

*

But there are other theories—says the mind
Of the mind. No ball of wax
Into which the falling leaves fall and leave Memory:
Always a world, never the—.
There are the birds:
                              The do-not-touch-me-
For-I-am-not-yours scarlet tanager—.
The wound-I-bear-I-do-not-feel rose-breasted
Grosbeak—. The who-clasped-around-my-neck-
This-chain-if-not-God dove—. The I-carry-the-sun-
On-my-back bobolink—. The I-wear-the-sun-
Between-my-eyes white-throated sparrow—.
Oriole that weaves a tear from tufts of deer
And thistle down—. Hermit thrush who cries
Inside her song—. There are the
                              Birds.
Each a body. Each a kind of knowledge
Flying through the columbarium

And to catch one is to know. Know what?
Something otherwise

                        Forgotten. What is good—.
What is love—. What is the geometric proof
Of God or love written on the dusky wing
Of the mourning dove—.

                       Ethics scratches
For grubs in the dust in which it bathes—.
The pigeon's red foot—. Aren't there

                           Others?—
Other wounds flying through the air—

                           Other
Wonders than honor in war and words worse
Than rage—

            The broken gold gears
In the blue jay's throat—

                The crow that dares
The kid with a BB gun to shoot—.

                    But shouldn't we
Imagine there are other kinds of birds, birds
Of ignorance flying about the soul with those others?—
Flying about those woods?—

                Nesting in nothing
But the hand that cups it, catches it—

                Sings a song
Called oblivion—

        Gives what cannot be taught
But only caught

        Blank behind the eye—
The empty vault—

        The un-thought—.

ACKNOWLEDGMENTS

Thank you to the editors of the following journals for publishing some of these poems: *2 Bridges Review, BOMB, Cincinnati Review, Crazyhorse, Dia12, Poetry, Harvard Review, High Country News, Here, Flag + Void, Under a Warm Green Linden, Seattle Review, New England Review,* and *The Volta.*

Abundant gratitude to Piotr Florczyk and K. A. Wisniewski of Textshop Editions for making a standalone chapbook of *Library Of*— and the vital vision of their press. Thank you to Del Harrow, Marius Lehene, and Mai Wagner for the artworks that grace those pages.

Thank you to Jeffrey Levine for keen-eyed advice on *Library Of*—, and for many years of the same for many other poems. Thank you to Bruce Bond, G. C. Waldrep, Kylan Rice, and Laynie Browne for reading and guidance. Thank you to Bruce Beasley and David Baker for the care and attention. To my dear colleagues and friends, Matthew Cooperman, Aby Kaupang, Sasha Steensen, and Camille Dungy. And to my friends with whom I've shared poems my whole writing life, Sally Keith and Srikanth Reddy.

And thank you, again, and ever more deeply, Del Harrow, for making art to grace the cover of this book.